"Aaaaaaaaaaaah!" screamed Algie.

The ghost was huge. It seemed to float above the ground. It flew toward Algie at top speed.

Algie swerved. He began to pedal as fast as he could.

He felt a swoosh of icy ghost air as the headless apparition reached for him.

Algie didn't dare look. He kept his head down and kept pedaling.

The ghost floated alongside him.

Algie pedaled faster.

The ghost stayed right with him.

They went over the bridge side by side.

And then, suddenly, the ghost wasn't there. The monstrous glowing white thing with no head was gone. . . .

Other Skylark Books you won't want to miss!

GRAVEYARD SCHOOL

The Headless Bicycle Rider

Tom B. Stone

A SKYLARK BOOK
Toronto New York London Sydney Auckland

RL 3.6, 008–012

THE HEADLESS BICYCLE RIDER
A Skylark Book / November 1994

Skylark Books is a registered trademark of Bantam Books,
a division of Bantam Doubleday Dell Publishing Group, Inc.
Registered in U.S. Patent and Trademark Office and elsewhere.

Graveyard School is a registered trademark of
Bantam Doubleday Dell Publishing Group, Inc.

ISBN 0-553-48225-4

Published simultaneously in the United States and Canada

*Bantam Books are published by Bantam Books, a division of
Bantam Doubleday Dell Publishing Group, Inc. Its trademark,
consisting of the words "Bantam Books" and the portrayal of a rooster,
is Registered in U.S. Patent and Trademark Office and in
other countries. Marca Registrada. Bantam Books,
1540 Broadway, New York, New York, 10036.*

PRINTED IN THE UNITED STATES OF AMERICA

OPM 0 9 8 7 6 5 4

GRAVEYARD SCHOOL

The Headless Bicycle Rider

CHAPTER

1

"Who's the new kid?" asked Jason Dunnbar loudly. He pointed at the door of the lunchroom and made a nerd-kid face.

All the boys sitting at his table in the Grove Hill Elementary School lunchroom laughed. All the girls sitting at the table nearby laughed, too.

Jason Dunnbar was probably the most popular kid at Grove. He had been class president since first grade, and he was also the star quarterback of the football team. Everybody liked Jason—because everyone had to. Those who didn't like him knew enough to keep quiet.

Because Jason was also the biggest kid in the school.

The new kid standing in the doorway looked as if he would be one of the kids who were smart enough to keep quiet. He was smaller than the average kid, and he wore big glasses and baggy jeans. His slightly too-long hair was pulled back in a stubby ponytail. His friendly expression grew even more friendly when Jason got up and walked over to him. But Jason didn't look at all interested in being friends. The new kid's expression changed to curiosity as he gazed down at the finger that Jason stuck into his chest.

"Who're you?" demanded Jason.

A small, anticipatory hush fell over Jason's table.

The kid squinted down at Jason's finger, then squinted back up at Jason. "Hello," the kid said, "I'm Algernon Green. Most people call me Algie. I'm new at Grove School. Today is my first day. I was a little late arriving this morning."

"Algernon?" asked Jason. "*Algie?*"

"Yes. How do you do?" Algie stuck his hand out. When Jason didn't stick his hand out also, Algie grabbed Jason's finger and removed it from his chest with a hearty handshake.

Kirstin Bjorg, who was sitting at the table of girls next to Jason's, shook her head so that her long blond hair swished over her shoulders. "This new guy just doesn't *get* it," she said.

"Get what?" asked Ken Dahl from his seat at the end of Jason's table.

Kirstin rolled her eyes. Ken didn't get it either. He was cute, but he was D-U-M-B.

Jason jerked his finger free of Algie's handshake. He frowned. He said, "I'm the class president. Welcome to Graveyard School."

2

It was Algie's turn to frown. "Graveyard School?" He squinted up at Jason. He pushed his glasses up his nose, then looked around the lunchroom. As he did, his gaze passed over the windows that looked out over the old graveyard on the hill above Grove School. It was the old graveyard—and some very weird and frightening happenings—that gave the school its nickname.

The frown left Algernon's face. He nodded. "Ah."

Maybe he does get it, Kirstin thought.

Jason turned away impatiently. His audience was waiting. "You want a place to sit for lunch?" he snapped.

Algie started to nod but stopped. He cleared his throat. "Sure."

"Good. I'll save you one. I'm sitting right over there." Jason pointed to his empty chair at the center of the table.

"Thank you," said Algie. He sniffed the air. "From the smell it doesn't appear that I will be eating much lunch."

Jason sauntered back over to the table. "Did'ja hear his name? What a jerk! He sounds like some science experiment!"

Several people snickered. Kirstin didn't. She thought there was something nice about Algie. Plus she wasn't afraid of Jason. Most of the time, she thought he was funny, just the way everybody else did. But when she didn't, she didn't feel as if she had to laugh anyway. As the sweeper and captain of the soccer team, she was fearless. She wasn't going to be afraid of someone as lame as Jason.

She watched Algie Green as he talked to one of the lunchroom workers dishing up the goop from the caf line. *What a weird name for a kid,* she thought. Parents got away with too much sometimes.

She looked on as Algie picked up his tray and made his way carefully across the lunchroom. When he reached Jason's table, he stopped.

Algernon Green didn't like what he saw. A whole tableful of kids his age were looking back at him. He knew what those looks meant; he had seen them before.

They were waiting to see what would happen next. They were waiting to be entertained.

And Algie knew he would be the entertainment.

I might as well get it over with, he thought, taking a deep breath.

The lunchroom had gotten so quiet you could hear a fork drop. "Hi," Algie said finally, breaking the eerie silence.

"Well, hello," answered Jason with a mocking sneer.

Someone giggled.

No doubt about it. Everybody in the lunchroom was watching. What happened to Algie at this table now would determine his fate for the rest of the year at Graveyard School. And possibly the rest of his life.

"Your table appears to be full," said Algie. "So I'll find my own place. Thank you."

He turned away.

Kirstin's mouth dropped open. Whoa! The little shrimp had actually made Jason look dumb!

And he *almost* got away with it.

"Hey!" Jason suddenly said. "Hey, you! Algie. Come back! You can have *my* seat."

Algie looked over his shoulder, an inquiring and almost sheeplike expression on his face.

Kirstin was disappointed. The new kid hadn't even realized what he was doing. He hadn't meant to stand up to Jason. It had just been an accident.

"C'mere!" ordered Jason.

Algie turned around and walked reluctantly back toward the table.

Jason stepped to one side. With a big grin he pulled his chair out. "Siddown," he said.

Trying not to be obvious, Algie quickly inspected the chair. Nothing disgusting was spread across the seat.

He put his tray down on the table. He glanced around the table. Everyone was watching expectantly. It made him feel like the prize turkey right before Thanksgiving.

Algie looked over his shoulder at Jason. Jason wiped the grin of anticipation off his face.

"Where will you sit?" Algie asked, stalling for time.

"Don't worry about me," answered Jason.

Algie gave up.

He almost sat down. He actually fell down. Jason had pulled the chair out from under him.

As Algie crashed to the lunchroom floor, everyone in the lunchroom began to laugh.

Algie studied the underside of the table for a moment, waiting for the laughter to die down. He counted to ten, using wads of gum stuck around the bottom edge of the tabletop.

Then he got up. "Thanks," he said. He picked up his tray and walked quickly away.

The laughter continued for a while as, alone and embarrassed, Algie ate his lunch. He couldn't believe he'd fallen for Jason's dumb joke. It seemed that in every school he was at he ended up the class geek.

Algie *had* moved a lot; he'd never been in the same school for a whole year. He was tired of being the new kid—the *weird* new kid. He was tired of being teased and picked on, just like Clark Kent. But although he was tired of the same old label, Algie knew there was nothing he could do. He was doomed to geekdom. Forever.

And unfortunately, unlike Clark Kent, he couldn't just go into a telephone booth and change into Superman. He couldn't come out and pound Jason to a pulp.

He had to abide by the rules of the real world, and Algie Green had to keep on being Algie Green.

He'd just have to wait until Jason and his friends got tired of picking on him—just like in every other school. Algie sighed. He hoped he wouldn't have to wait too long.

CHAPTER

2

"How'd it go, dear?" asked Mrs. Green as Algie trudged wearily through the door that afternoon.

Algie shrugged. He put his lunch in its plain brown paper bag on the counter.

"You didn't eat your lunch?" asked his mother.

"Kids here don't *bring* their lunches, they *buy* them," said Algie. "So I bought mine. I was trying to blend in."

His mother made a face. "Did it work?"

Algie shrugged.

"It'll get better," said his mother.

Algie shrugged again.

"It will," said his mom. "Don't let it bother you. You've got a good head on your shoulders."

"Yeah, Mom," said Algie. He rolled his eyes and headed up the stairs.

A lot of the stuff in his room was still in boxes. He was trying to decide whether to unpack or just shove the unopened boxes under his bed until he needed them. Would his parents count putting the boxes under the bed as cleaning his room?

He dumped his backpack on the floor by the door. He took off his shoes and socks. "Phew," said Algie, and slid the socks under the bed.

Flipping on his computer, he sat down and tilted his chair back and lifted his feet to the mouse. He was trying to learn to play computer games with his toes. He'd read about a famous magician, Houdini, who'd been able to write and untie knots and do all kinds of other tricks with his toes. It had seemed like a useful skill.

But so far Algie was awful at playing computer games with his feet. He could tell it would be a long time before he graduated to tying and untying knots.

He kept practicing, although the computer beat him time after time. After a while his feet got tired. He sat up and used his hands. He beat the computer six times and got bored and quit.

He flopped back across the bed and stared at the ceiling.

Beating the computer was no fun. What he'd like to do was beat that jerk Jason.

It hadn't been an easy day. Jason's chair trick had been just the beginning. He'd also tripped Algie as Algie had walked by in math class. He'd done something—Algie wasn't sure what—to make the whole class laugh when Algie had been called on in English.

And I wasn't even there a whole day, thought Algie in despair.

Walking up to Graveyard School the next morning was almost as scary as being the new kid walking into the lunchroom. As Algie approached the broad shallow steps leading up to the front door of the school, he noticed that the kids on the steps seemed to be arranged in a certain order. The littlest kids were at the bottom, and the sixth graders were at the top. He trudged through all the kids. When he reached the top, a movement behind the glass panel of the front door caught his eye. He thought he recognized the principal, Dr. Morthouse, from his welcome-to-Grove-School visit to the office the morning before.

He'd thought she was pretty spooky then. He was even more sure of it now. Why would a principal lurk behind the doors of the school before it started?

It gave him the creeps.

He shifted his pack to his other shoulder. A voice said, "Hey, watch it!"

Algie turned quickly in case it was Jason. It wasn't. It was the blond girl he had noticed sitting at the table near Jason's at lunch the day before.

"Hello," he said cautiously. She didn't look unfriendly. But he couldn't be too careful.

"Hi," she said. "How do you like it?"

"Grove School . . . I mean, Graveyard School?"

"Yeah. That." Her blue eyes beneath her bangs were cool but not mean.

She seemed sure of herself, and Algie decided that she had never been picked on by Jason or anyone else in her life.

"School's okay," he said, feeling more at ease.

"Really," the girl said, then smiled. "I'm Kirstin Bjorg."

"I'm—"

"Algie Green," she finished for him. "That's a weird name."

"My parents picked it. They *are* kind of weird," admitted Algie.

"Whose aren't?" She laughed and waved over a group of kids who had been standing nearby. "Algie, this is Park, Jaws, Skate, Vickie, and Stacey. Park likes baseball. Skate and Vickie are, like, boardheads." She paused, then nodded toward a round boy who was chewing rapidly. "That's Jaws. Jaws'll eat anything."

"Even road kill," said Jaws proudly in mid-chew.

"And Stacey is a world class dog walker and money-maker—"

"Really?" Algie interrupted this time. "I have my own paper route. I just got it. I'm trying to earn money for—well, I like having money."

No one spoke for a minute. *Great*, thought Algie. *It's probably another rule, like don't bring your lunch and don't stand in the wrong place on the steps.* No paper routes for the Graveyard Hill students.

Then Vickie said, "You use a skateboard to do it? Your route?"

Algie shook his head. "I don't know how. I just use my bike."

"Oh," said Vickie, "you should try a board. They're excellent."

"Morning route?" asked Kirstin, as if she weren't really listening.

"Afternoons. After school."

"Guess you won't be playing any sports, like baseball," said Park.

"Baseball's not until next spring," said Algie. "Maybe I could do a morning route by then."

Park nodded. "True."

At that moment the bell rang.

"Time to go," said Stacey. "Listen, I'll check with some of my dog-walking customers and see if they want an afternoon paper."

"Thanks," said Algie.

Could it be that he was actually making friends? He went into the school feeling much better than he had when he arrived.

But that didn't last long.

11

Algie wasn't expecting what happened next.

He opened his locker. Someone called his name. It was Jason.

"Hey, Algie!" said Jason. He sounded friendly—and completely phony. Someone came up to the locker next to Algie's. But Algie was keeping a wary eye on Jason.

"Hey, you're not mad at me, are you?" asked Jason. He stuck out his hand for a shake. "No hard feelings."

Algie frowned at Jason. What was he up to? Maybe he really *did* want to be friends. Algie tentatively stuck his hand out.

Jason shook it and left. "Remember—no hard feelings, man."

Algie waved and sighed with relief. Maybe things were going to work out at Graveyard School. He smiled to himself as he reached into his locker. His expression suddenly changed.

"AaaaaaaahhhHHHH!" he screamed.

CHAPTER
3

A huge rat came wiggling out of Algie's locker. It caught Algie's hand. Algie leaped back, shaking his whole arm frantically.

"AAaAh! Auuuaw! Aaaaaaa!" he screamed.

The rat's body flew off and hit the wall with a thud. It slid down and lay lifelessly on the floor.

"Euuuuw!" a girl shouted. "A *rat!* A rat!"

Suddenly everybody in the hall was screaming and running and pushing.

Except Jason and his friends. From a safe distance a little farther down the hall, they'd stopped and were doubled over with laughter.

Algie stopped trying not to scream. He pushed his glasses up his nose to give himself time to think. He looked down the hall at Jason.

Then he looked over at the rat. For a moment he thought he was going to be sick.

Jason straightened up and gave the boy next to him a high five. Algie recognized the boy. He'd come up to the locker next to Algie's while Algie was talking to Jason.

That must have been when they slipped the rat in, thought Algie in disgust.

The screaming stopped abruptly. The students parted like the sea.

Dr. Morthouse was bearing down on Algie.

"What's going on here?" she demanded. She had a voice that made fingernails on blackboards sound good.

"Ah," said Algie. "Well . . ."

"Someone left a fake rat in his locker," a girl's voice said at Algie's shoulder. Algie turned. Kirstin had come up to stand beside him.

Dr. Morthouse gave Kirstin an evil look. But Kirstin didn't seem to notice. Or to care.

Kirstin pointed to the rat that was lying against the wall. Algie walked cautiously toward it, followed by Dr. Morthouse and Kirstin.

As he got closer, Algie could see the rat was a fake one, a very realistic fake one. It had little eyes made of red plastic and shaggy fur and long rat teeth.

Algie hated rats.

Dr. Morthouse folded her arms. She grimaced. Something silver glinted in her mouth.

"I'll get it," said Algie quickly. He made himself pick up the rat and hold it up by the tail.

Dr. Morthouse unfolded her arms, reached, and took

14

the rat out of Algie's hand with her thumb and forefinger. She held it up by its neck.

"If this is your way of getting attention or making friends at a new school, Algernon, let me suggest that you abandon that course of action."

"What?" said Algie. He was stunned.

"And if it is someone else's idea of a joke"—Dr. Morthouse raised her voice and looked around at the few students brave enough to have stayed in the hall—"then let me tell you, I am *not* amused."

She turned and stalked down the hall, holding the rat by the neck. The way she was holding it made Algie shudder. *If that had been a live rat, it'd be a dead rat now,* he thought. Aloud he said, "I didn't do anything. I never saw that rat before in my life!"

"No," said Kirstin. "But you sure screamed."

"Yeah," said Algie glumly. He bent over and picked up his notebook from where he had flung it on the floor. He stuffed it into his pack and went back to his locker and slammed it shut.

He was surprised to find Kirstin still standing there when he turned around. She fell into step next to Algie, and they walked down the hall.

At the door of the classroom Jason was leaning against the wall. He straightened up. "Good one, huh, Algie? Craig and I really got you."

"Yes," answered Algie crossly.

"Hey, you're not going to hold it against me, are you?"

15

Algie didn't answer.

"Hey, forgive me. But it was such a good idea. I mean, you should have heard you scream. And that jump? Like you were taking a shot at the moon."

Craig laughed. Several other students hanging out in the hall around the door began to laugh, too.

"It was a stupid joke," said Kirstin.

Jason stopped in mid-laugh. "What?"

Two girls sitting on the front row of the class began to giggle. Jason gave them a quick glare, then focused on Kirstin. "What did you say?"

"I said it was a stupid joke," Kirstin repeated. She brushed past Jason and went to her seat.

"Whoa, Jason, she told you," said Craig.

"Ha-ha," said Jason in a nasty voice. He looked at Algie, who was still standing in the doorway.

"What're you looking at, *Algernon*?" Jason snarled.

"Nothing," said Algie, and walked quickly to his seat as the teacher stood up and called the class to order.

Sliding into his seat, Algie could feel Jason giving him the evil eye. *I wonder how many kids like me have gotten buried alive at Graveyard School?* he silently worried.

The day went downhill from there. When the teacher called on Algie in math, Algie got the answer right. He couldn't help himself.

He couldn't help flinching, either, when he heard Jason muttering, "Teacher's pet, teacher's pet."

At lunch, as Algie walked by, Jason and his friends burst into laughter. "Going to sit with the *girls*, Algie. Going to sit with your *girlfriend*?" Jason taunted.

"No—" began Algie.

But before he could go on, Kirstin leaped to her feet, her blue eyes flashing. "Shut up, Jason!"

Jason kept laughing. "Hey, Algie," he said, "your girlfriend wants me to shut up. What should I dooooo?"

Jason and all the boys laughed even more loudly.

"Over here," said a voice. Algie walked quickly toward it and sat down gratefully. A moment later he realized it was Park Addams and Jaws Bennett. Jaws was chewing at top speed. Somehow Algie wasn't surprised.

"Hi," said Algie.

"You want your lunch?" asked Jaws.

"Uh, I don't know yet," answered Algie.

"Let me know. Anything you don't want, I get first dibs."

"Right," said Algie.

A few minutes later Stacey and another girl, who had dark hair and bangs that stuck up, came and sat down at the table.

"This is Maria Medina," said Stacey. Maria said a soft hi, but then the two girls made faces as they noticed perfect Polly Hannah walking toward their table.

17

Polly walked as if she were on stage in front of hundreds of people, her head held high, her nose in the air.

"Someday it's gonna rain and your nose is gonna fill up with water and you're going to drown, Polly," said Maria.

Stacey and Park started laughing. Polly ignored them. She put her tray down. She tucked in her shirt. She smoothed her skirt and inspected the seat of the chair carefully. Then she sat down.

Algie wondered if anyone had ever pulled a chair out from under Polly. He filed the idea away in his brain for future reference.

"Polly, this is Algie. Algie, Polly."

"I know," said Polly. She smiled a small, satisfied smile. "We all saw you yesterday. When Jason creamed you with the chair trick."

Algie felt his face turn red.

"Great, Polly," said Maria in disgust. She pushed her dark bangs back so they were standing straight up in spikes and turned to Algie. "Where're you from?"

"It's a long story," said Algie. "I've moved a lot."

"Too bad," said Polly. The way she said it didn't sound sympathetic at all.

"Algie has a paper route," Stacey pointed out, to change the subject.

"Yeah. Afternoons after school. Just weekdays. Someone else does the weekends."

"Good deal," said Jaws, between bites.

"It's nice to have money," said Stacey. "I mean, my parents' idea of an allowance is so feeble."

"Well, I'm not going to get rich delivering papers," said Algie. "At least not unless I get some new customers."

"Good luck," said Polly. She looked over at Jason's table. She smiled. "You're going to need it."

Algie thought about Polly's words as he delivered his papers that afternoon. She'd meant just the opposite of what she'd said. But it was true. He was going to need some luck.

He wasn't sure he could take a whole year of Jason's nasty jokes. Jason *might* get tired of picking on him after a while. But somehow Algie didn't think so.

He reached into his basket and slung a newspaper far up a front walk. It landed right in the middle of the front doormat.

Maybe I'll try out for baseball this spring, thought Algie. *If I'm still around.*

If Jason hasn't killed me.

Algie wished he could fight back. But he couldn't. At least, not really.

But maybe he could think of something.

Thump. Another paper right on target.

He spent the rest of the paper route imagining that he

was aiming the paper at Jason's face. It improved his aim considerably.

And the job went much faster. Before he knew it, he was finished for the day.

Maybe it hadn't been such a bad day after all.

And who knew when his luck would change?

CHAPTER
4

The letter was waiting for him when he got home. It came in a plain white envelope. His name and address were printed on the front in block letters in black ink. In the upper-right-hand corner the return address listed the name K. Bates and an address on Seven Mile Hollow Road.

Algie took the letter with him up to his room. He sat down at his desk and tore open the envelope.

He took out a single sheet of paper and unfolded it. On it were the typewritten words "For delivery of the daily paper *precisely* at 4:45 P.M. to the front steps of my house every weekday. Do Not Be Early. Do Not Be Late.

"Do Not Linger."

"Creepy," muttered Algie. Then he realized that something else was inside the envelope.

A sheaf of new bills fell out. A stash of cash. A wad of money.

"Wow!" Algie couldn't believe his eyes. From past experience with paper routes, he knew that while some customers actually paid their bills on time, most bought their newspapers on the buy now, pay later plan. That meant that Algie delivered the newspapers and billed the customer. As the bills got bigger, Algie got more and more nervous. Sooner or later he found himself doing the thing he hated doing most of all: standing at someone's front door, holding a copy of the bill and asking the person—as if he or she were doing *him* a favor—to please pay him the money owed him.

People always acted as if it were a big surprise.

They always paid by check.

And sometimes the checks weren't even any good.

He had hardly ever been paid in cash. And he had never, ever been paid in advance.

But that's what this had to be. A *huge* payment in advance. Algie looked down at the sheet of paper. Sure enough, at the bottom it said: "P.S. Payment in advance included herewith."

"Decent," said Algie. His luck, he decided, had definitely changed. He reached under the bed and pulled out his bank. It was a flat metal box with a lock and key. Algie kept his most valuable possessions in the box.

He put the stack of bills in the corner of the box. They looked nice and green in there with all the other stuff.

"Decent," said Algie again. Whoever this K. Bates was, he—or she—was okay by Algie.

He locked the box and shoved it back under his bed.

"You're kidding!" Park Addams said the next day. He grabbed his throat with both hands and made a gagging sound.

"No," said Algie. "Why would I be?"

"You got an actual letter from old Mr. Bates?"

"You know him?"

Park let go of his throat and laughed aloud. "Know *him*? Not me! You couldn't pay me to shake his hand."

"Park!" Jason fired a basketball in Park's direction. Park caught it and winged it back.

"Later," he called to Jason.

It was recess. Park and Algie were standing at the edge of a basketball game among Jason and most of the other sixth-grade boys. Nearby, members of the girls' and boys' soccer teams were scrimmaging. Park, as always, had his baseball glove stuffed in his hip pocket.

Algie had just told Park about his new newspaper route client. He'd been hoping Park could tell him where Seven Mile Hollow Road was. He hadn't been expecting Park's reaction at all.

"What's wrong with Mr. Bates?" said Algie.

Park looked over his shoulder. Then he stepped a little closer to Algie and lowered his voice. "What's wrong with

Mr. Bates? *What's wrong with Mr. Bates?* I'll tell you what's wrong with Mr. Bates! He's an *ax murderer!*"

Algie grew completely disgusted with Park. "Yeah, right, Park. Thanks for your help." He turned to walk away.

"Heads up, Green!" Suddenly a basketball came out of nowhere. Algie threw up his hand at the last minute. The ball bounced off his fingers and flew up into his face.

Algie staggered backward. His glasses flew in the air.

For the second time in two weeks Algie felt the eyes of a large group of students on him. This time it was all the students on the playground.

"Gee, Algernon, are you all right?" Jason sang.

Algie squinted in the direction of Jason's voice. He could barely make out Jason's shape. Without his glasses Algie could barely see two feet in front of his nose.

Now he had to find his glasses before someone stepped on them.

But it was already too late. As Algie crouched down and groped on the ground, he found his glasses—in two pieces. They'd broken at the nose.

"I guess I shouldn't throw passes at boys who wear glasses," said Jason as Algie stood slowly up.

Jason began to laugh, and other voices joined in.

With a sigh Algie turned back in the general direction of the school.

"Too bad," said Park at his shoulder.

Then another voice spoke by his elbow. "I have some

24

electrical tape in my locker," Kirstin said. "I use it on my lucky soccer cleats. They're falling apart."

"I could use that to tape my glasses together," said Algie gratefully.

The three of them began to walk back toward the school. As they reached the top of the stairs, they ran into Mr. Lucre, the assistant principal.

"Boys and girls—or I should say girl. Or I could say Kirstin, since I know your name—"

"Hello, Mr. Lucre," said Kirstin.

"Where are you going, boys and gir—er, Kirstin?"

"To my locker," said Kirstin. "To get some tape to tape Algie's glasses back together."

"Oh, dear. An accident?"

"Well, I didn't do it on purpose," said Algie.

"Just a basketball thing," said Park quickly.

"Oh. Well, hurry up. You don't want to miss your exercise period." Even without his glasses, Algie could see the assistant principal rubbing his plump hands together.

"Right," said Park, grabbing Algie's shirtsleeve and pulling him around Mr. Lucre and into the building.

"Mr. Lucre's a space cadet," said Algie.

"That's nothing," said Kirstin. "You wouldn't believe some of the people around this school."

"Yeah, right," said Algie. "They're all ax murderers."

Kirstin stopped and opened her locker. She searched inside for a moment and then pulled out a roll of silver electrical tape and handed it to Algie. With the speed of

25

long practice, Algie began to tape his glasses back together.

He finished. The tape made a big silver lump where it held the glasses together on his nose. It made him feel like a dweeb rhinoceros. But Kirstin didn't seem to notice. She just took the tape and dropped it back on the floor of her locker.

As she slammed the locker and turned back around, Kirstin finished Algie's earlier thought. "Ax murders? No. Not in our school. The only ax murderer is old Mr. Bates, who lives out on Seven Mile Hollow Road."

CHAPTER
5

Slowly Algie took his glasses off, as if they had some-how affected his hearing. He put them back on. He pushed them up his nose.

He stared at Kirstin.

Then he turned to stare at Park.

"I told you so," Park said smugly.

"I don't believe it," said Algie.

"You've heard about Mr. Bates?" asked Kirstin. She led the way down the hall toward the door to the play-ground. With his glasses on, Algie could see Mr. Lucre, still hovering in the doorway, still rubbing his hands to-gether.

"No. I mean, yes. I mean, I just got him for my paper route."

Kirstin stopped in her tracks. She stared at Algie. "Mr. *Korman Bates*? Are you sure?"

"Kirstin, keep walking," Park said. "If you act weird,

Mr. Lucre will come down here and start talking to us and telling us he's our friend."

"Oh, yeah. Right." Kirstin started forward again. The three headed slowly out the door. When they'd gotten past Mr. Lucre and back to the playground, Kirstin repeated, "Are you sure? You got Mr. Korman Bates for a customer?"

"In cash," answered Algie, and told the two about the letter.

Park said, "I wouldn't take that job even for money. What if he cuts off your head when you deliver the paper?"

"How do you know he's an ax murderer?" asked Algie. "Was it in the newspapers? Was his face on the most wanted signs at the post office?"

"Everybody just knows it," said Park. "The way they know the sun rises in the east or something."

"It's not the same thing," argued Algie. "Who did he ax out? When? Was he in jail? Why isn't he in jail now?"

Kirstin seemed to have stopped listening to them. She was staring out at the basketball game, watching Jason sink hoop after hoop. She was frowning.

"Just the way everyone knows the road to Mr. Bates's house is haunted," Park said.

"What?" *Great,* thought Algie, *this is all I need.*

"His victims haunt the road. They go up and down it and spring out on unwary passersby, saying, 'Give me back my headdddddd,' " Park told Algie.

Kirstin turned her head slowly. She said, "I never heard that the ghost talked. And why would it say that? I mean, why would some complete stranger have its head? And why would a ghost need a head anyway?"

"I knew you were making this all up," said Algie to both of them in disgust. To his relief the bell rang. He turned to go back inside.

"No! Wait. I'm serious," cried Park.

"Forget it," said Algie. "Jason can get me—*sometimes*—with his dumb jokes. But not you."

"But it's true!"

"I'll believe it when I see it," said Algie, and kept walking.

"And then what?" Park called after him. "When the ghost comes up and tries to grab your head for himself, then what are you going to do?"

Thump, squeak, squeak, squeak, squeak, thump, squeak, squeak, squeak . . .

Algie finished his paper route to the tune of a squeaky wheel. He wished he had a better bike. A cool, fast bike that could handle roads and do cross-country trails. An all-terrain bike that could leap rocks and curbs and fallen trees at a single bound.

He was going to use some of his money for a new bike someday. As a sort of business expense.

Thump, squeak, squeak, squeak . . .

The squeaking continued without interruption now.

He had only one more paper to deliver—to his newest customer, Mr. Bates.

Grove Hill was just an ordinary, average-size town. Algie lived on one edge of it, the edge near Graveyard School. The school had been built on Grove Hill Road when the town had been expected to grow. Only Grove Hill had never grown. It had never changed. It had stayed just the same.

Seven Mile Hollow Road was an old road of pitted, potholed tar off Grove on the same end of town as the school. As it turned off Grove Hill Road beyond the school, it began as a narrow two-lane blacktop that went past a few small farms. As it wound farther and farther away from town, Seven Mile Hollow Road became more and more beat up and worn out. The tar was replaced by dirt and rocks and big ruts. The farmers' fields that lined the road gave way to overgrown pastures and then to woods and a swamp.

Algie had never been on Seven Mile Hollow Road, but he had made sure he gave himself plenty of time to deliver Mr. Bates's paper. After what Park had said, he wasn't about to get caught anywhere near Mr. Bates's place after dark.

Just because he didn't believe Park didn't mean he needed to take any chances, he told himself.

He was glad he'd planned ahead. He didn't like the way the road kept getting narrower and narrower. He didn't like the way the trees seemed to lean farther and farther over. He didn't like the way his bike kept squeaking.

Squeak, squeak, squeak. Nothing silent about his approach through the chilly, silent woods that pressed against the road. He pedaled up and over an old bridge above a dry creek bed. The boards on the bridge groaned and creaked as Algie went over. Looking down, he noticed that one of the boards was missing.

He looked quickly back up. The rocky creek bed had looked as if it were miles and miles down. On the other side of the bridge Algie stopped.

The road ahead was even narrower and darker than the road he'd left behind. Algie peered through the tunnel of trees.

I don't like this either, he thought. *I don't like this one bit.*

He looked over his shoulder. Nothing was behind him. He looked up at the sky, just to be sure. Yep. Plenty of daylight left.

He took a deep breath. Even if Mr. Bates was some kind of crazy ax murderer, he wasn't going to chase Algie. Why should he? All Algie was doing was delivering the paper.

Besides, he'd left a big note at home, so his parents would know where he was, just in case.

No reason to take any chances.

"This is stupid," said Algie aloud. He got back on his bike. He felt the newspaper bump against him in the backpack. All he had to do was find the house, ride part-way toward it, give the paper a good, accurate heave toward the front doormat, and take off.

No problem. Piece of cake. Why worry?

He was so intent on his thoughts that he almost ran into the huge wooden gate at the end of the road.

He looked up and saw it and swerved at the last minute. He almost fell off his bike.

DEAD END, read a sign nailed to a dead tree by the gate. On the gate was another sign: NO TRESPASSING. DO NOT ENTER. GO AWAY.

At the bottom of the sign, in smaller letters, it said K. BATES.

Algie gulped. He pushed his bike closer and peered through the weathered gray boards of the gate. The road on the other side wasn't much more than a weedy trail. Algie could tell that no one had driven that way in a long, long time.

"The way I see it, Algie," he said aloud, "you have two choices: deliver the paper or mail back the money."

He didn't want to deliver the paper. But he didn't want to mail back the money either.

Algie sighed. He looked at his watch. It was 4:45 P.M.

"Every man has his price," he said. "When I get older, mine's going to be a lot higher."

He pushed open the gate, got on his bike, and headed down K. Bates's driveway.

It was a world-record terrible driveway. Ruts grabbed at his wheels. Weeds slapped at his legs. Branches scraped at his face.

And it was dark. Much darker beneath the trees along the driveway than it had been even along the road.

Algie gritted his teeth and pedaled on. He was a professional, he reminded himself. There wasn't a paper he couldn't deliver, a customer he couldn't handle.

Without warning, the road dipped steeply.

"Whoooooooooooaaaaaa," cried Algie. He slammed on the brakes so hard that he almost pitched headfirst over the handlebars. The bike skidded to a halt, and Algie fell off sideways onto the dirt.

He'd reached the house.

It had definite haunted house possibilities: It was old and sagging and needed paint. Shutters were pulled shut across some of the windows. The others had faded curtains drawn across them. Three splintery steps led up to a narrow splintery porch that seemed much too small for the massive, pitch-black front door.

As Algie scrambled to his hands and knees, something moved in the garden.

He straightened up. His eyes widened.

A ragged figure stood there, its massive balloon-shaped head lolling to one side as if its neck were broken. Fat arms flapped from its huge, hunched shoulders. A maniacal grin leered from its pale face.

33

And a huge, evil black bird perched on its shoulder.

Suddenly the bird flew up in the air. It circled once and then swooped down at Algie.

"Eeeeeeeeeeeeerrrrrawwwwww!" it screamed, its red eyes blazing.

CHAPTER

6

Algie screamed. He grabbed the newspaper in his pack and flung it at the shrieking bird. The bird swerved and flapped heavily up into the air and away.

"Caw, caw, caw," it called mockingly as it disappeared into the darkness of the trees.

Algie whirled around to face Mr. Bates.

But no one was there.

Just an old, sagging scarecrow, its arms flapping in the wind.

Algie couldn't believe it. He'd been psyched out by a stupid scarecrow.

Quickly, his heart still pounding, he ran and scooped up the paper. He turned and threw a perfect newspaper slider pitch. The paper sailed through the air and landed on the front porch right in front of the door.

The sound echoed like a gunshot in the eerie stillness of the early evening.

"Forget it," said Algie. He wasn't waiting around to

see who—or what—opened the door to pick up the paper. He jumped on his bike and pedaled back up the driveway as fast as he could go. He didn't let up until he got over the bridge and back out to the main road.

He wasn't sure, but he thought, as he turned off Seven Mile Hollow and headed home, that he heard the faint mocking sound of a crow cawing overhead.

Algie sat in the school library. He had his back to the wall and the library table in front of him. No way was he letting Jason—or anyone else—sneak up on him.

Ever since he'd started delivering the paper to Mr. Bates the day before, he'd been a little jumpy. Not that anything had happened. The scarecrow had stayed in the garden. The crow had reappeared. And although he was sure that someone—or something—was watching him as he lurched down the driveway on his bicycle and hurled the paper onto the front porch from a safe distance, he hadn't seen anything yet.

Nothing except shadows and the odd shapes scurrying away into the woods.

At least worrying about his paper route was keeping his mind off Jason. And for some reason Jason had been taking it easy on Algie.

Until now.

"So, how's business?" Jason asked as he loomed over Algie's table.

"Business?" asked Algie. He looked up at Jason, then

casually looked past Jason's bulky body. Good. The librarian was on duty at the desk. She'd be able to see what Jason was up to before he inflicted too much bodily harm on Algie. If both the librarian and Algie screamed, help might even come in time to save him.

"The paper business," said Jason.

"Fine," said Algie.

"Good, good," said Jason heartily. For a moment he sounded weirdly like Mr. Lucre, trying to be friendly to all the students at Graveyard School.

A moment later Algie knew why Jason sounded so strange.

"I thought I'd let you know. I'm running for class president this year. Again."

"You've been president of the sixth grade before?" Algie asked before he could stop himself.

Jason frowned.

Algie made himself look innocent. He could almost see Jason thinking: *If I kill him now, he can't vote for me for class president.*

Jason said, "I was class president in fifth grade. And fourth. I've been class president at Graveyard School ever since first grade."

"Wow," said Algie.

"So I just wanted to let you know. So you can vote for me . . ." Jason paused. He looked around. He leaned over. "Things have been going pretty good for you the last few days, right?"

37

"Right," said Algie. He wanted to lean back. He wanted to get as far away from Jason as possible. But he forced himself to stay where he was.

Jason straightened up and grinned. "That's class leadership for you, Algernon. With me as president, everyone, even you, has it pretty good."

Vote for you or I die, thought Algie. *I get it.* He nodded. "Got it," he said.

"Good," said Jason. He laughed in what he probably thought was a friendly way. "Don't study too hard." Then he walked away.

Algie looked down at his book. In it was a picture of a squat, hairy man dressed in animal skins. The man had shaggy hair and little mean eyes and big animal jaws. At the caveman's feet was a dead animal. *"An early caveman,"* read the caption under the picture, *"and his dinner."*

"Neanderthal," muttered Algie when he was sure Jason was safely out of hearing range. He looked over at the librarian. She had her back to the room. Quickly Algie wrote in parentheses after the word *caveman* in the caption below the picture: "(JASON)".

He'd never written in a library book before. He wondered if he was about to start on a career of crime.

"Algie," said a female voice.

Algie jumped a mile. "I didn't do it!" he stammered, slamming the library book shut.

"Do what?" asked Kirstin, sitting down across from him.

"Ah . . . finish my report. On world history."

"Oh. What're you doing it on?"

Algie kept the book closed. "Prehistoric people. I'm focusing on, ah, Neanderthals."

Kirstin said, "I was thinking of doing my report on cave art. You know, those paintings that they find in the caves."

"Cool," said Algie.

"Yeah. Listen, Algie. I have a favor to ask you. You can say no if you want, but I hope you won't."

Had anyone ever said no to Kirstin? Algie wondered. He kind of doubted it. "What is it?" he asked.

"You know Jason's running for class president?"

Algie nodded.

"Well, I've decided to run, too. Jason doesn't deserve to be class president. He's starting to act like a real politician."

"Yeah, he's pretty disgusting these days," said Algie. "Not that I knew him before. But hey, no problem. You've got my vote and support." *Even if Jason does waste me,* he thought. It would be worth it to see Jason Dunnbar lose at something for once.

"Good," said Kirstin, as if Algie's risking his life to vote for her were no big deal. As if she expected it. "That's not the favor."

Algie began to get a bad feeling, the kind of bad feeling he'd gotten when he'd seen the signs on the gate at Old Man Bates's place. The kind of bad feeling he got when a customer opened the door and gave him a big, friendly, toothy smile.

Kirstin gave him a big, friendly, toothy smile.

"Uh-oh," said Algie aloud before he could stop himself.

"What I want you to do, Algie, is run my campaign for me. Help me think of ideas. Help me make posters. I know I've got the girls' vote. I want you to help me win the guys' vote. The thinking guys' vote."

"Me?" said Algie. His voice was higher than ultrasound. "Do you really think that's a good idea, Kirstin? I mean . . ."

"It's a great idea, Algie! Why don't you want to help me?"

'Cause I don't want to die, thought Algie. He looked helplessly around the library. A million books, and no answers.

He looked at Kirstin. Did she have more teeth than normal? Why did her smile look so predatory?

Didn't she care that if he said yes, he'd help her run for class president, he was going to die?

Kirstin kept on smiling, her blue eyes fixed on his face.

Algie cleared his throat. "Okay," he said.

"Great!" Kirstin jumped up from the library table and slapped Algie on the shoulder. "We'll meet at your house

Saturday afternoon to plan our campaign strategy." She slung her backpack on her shoulder and walked out of the library, whistling, in spite of the librarian's frown, and bobbing her head to the tune.

Algie's heart sank as he watched her go. Saturday. Day after tomorrow. At his house. He could just hear his mother talking about how great it was he was making friends. He could just hear his father making big, jolly jokes about Algie's new "girlfriend."

And he could just imagine what Jason was going to do to him when Jason found out.

Maybe, with any luck, Old Man Bates would have beheaded him by then. Beheading would be quick and painless compared with what Algie was facing now.

He opened the book again to the picture with the caption "An early caveman and his dinner." Without even checking to see if the librarian was looking, he wrote the word *Algie* in parentheses after the word *dinner*.

CHAPTER
7

"You're not thinking, Algie," said Kirstin in a disappointed voice.

"Yes, I am," said Algie.

"He's thinking about what Jason's going to do to him when he finds out he's your campaign manager," said Polly smugly. She was coloring in the second letter *i* in the word *Kirstin* on a poster she was working on. It said KIRSTIN FOR PRESIDENT.

It wasn't original, but it was neat.

"Algie can handle Jason," said Kirstin. "He's smarter than Jason."

"Not if he's dead," said Polly.

"Be quiet, Polly," said Maria. "Hey, Algie, speaking of dead, have you met old Mr. Bates yet?"

"No," said Algie. "But the ride to his house is pretty creepy. I still don't think he's an ax murderer, though."

"You wait until you see the headless ghost. Then you'll know it's true," said Park. He looked at his watch, then began to write on the poster quickly. He'd agreed to help Algie with the campaign, but not if it cut into his baseball playing time. Stacey was coming later in the afternoon, with some of Kirstin's best girlfriends. At the moment she was walking dogs.

Algie said, "Have you ever seen the ghost, Park?"

Park shook his head reluctantly. "Nope. But then, I don't hang out on Seven Mile Hollow Road. Nobody does."

"Then how do you know about Mr. Bates? Did the sheriff tell you? Was there an announcement in the newspaper when he moved to town?"

"Moved to town?" Polly frowned. "He didn't move to town. He's always lived there."

"If he's always lived there," said Algie, "then he beheaded someone else who lived around here. Who was it? When was it? Why didn't they arrest him and send him to prison?" Algie picked a bloodred marker and began to write the name KIRSTIN in big, bloody, slashing, angry letters on a piece of paper in front of him.

"Cool," said Kirstin.. She bent forward to study the lettering. "That would make a great sort of campaign logo, you know."

Polly, who was holding a pink Magic Marker, looked at the lettering and made a face.

"Well, Park?" Algie persisted.

Maria said, "My father said Mr. Bates used to own a motel out on the old highway. Then they built the

44

new road and the motel went out of business. My father said that the new road took all the business from Grove Hill and turned it into a small town again. My father says—"

"Did your father say Mr. Bates whacked someone's head off with an ax?" asked Algie.

"Nope."

"Someone at the hotel, see?" said Park. "No one knew they were missing 'cause they were traveling by themselves and they took a shortcut and got lost and it was late and they stopped there. And Mr. Bates was crazy because he didn't have any business anymore, and this person started complaining about the old road and saying how he should have stayed on the new road and Mr. Bates just lost it and *whack*."

In spite of himself, Algie jumped.

Kirstin said, "Park, you made that whole thing up."

"Yeah, but it could have happened," argued Park.

"Look, if there's a ghost along Seven Mile Hollow Road, maybe it doesn't have anything to do with Mr. Bates," said Kirstin.

"There isn't a ghost," said Algie. "I would have seen it by now, okay?"

"Maybe the ghost is waiting to catch you off guard," said Polly.

"Shut *up*," Algie said, surprising everyone, including himself.

• • •

On Monday at school Algie put the last piece of tape on the lower-right-hand corner of the poster. He stood back and regarded his work.

KIRSTIN FIRST, it said in big, red, slashing letters. Below, in smaller, block letters in black it said KIRSTIN FOR PRESIDENT. VOTE SMART.

"Who're you calling dumb?" snarled a voice in Algie's ear, startling him.

The hairs on Algie's neck stood up. Especially when the hand clamped onto his ponytail and yanked his head back.

It was hard, but Algie managed to turn around to face Jason.

"Nobody," Algie croaked. "I'm not calling anybody dumb."

"That's what you're saying, isn't it? That if you don't vote for *her*, you're stupid."

"No, not at all." *Yes, yes, yes, you big dumb Neanderthal.*

Could Jason read minds? In one instant his face went from nice, well-liked all-around sixth-grade guy to snarling . . . Neanderthal.

"You said you were gonna vote for me."

"Uh . . ."

"You had it good, Algernon. That's over now."

Algie was having trouble swallowing, because Jason had pulled his head so far back. He wished he were wearing a turtleneck. At least his neck wouldn't have felt so exposed.

"I'm gonna rip your head off, you little dweeb," snarled Jason, practically mashing his face against Algie's. Jason was so close that he was fogging up Algie's glasses.

"Uh . . . " Algie tried again.

"You boys gonna fight?" asked a gravelly voice.

Jason let go of Algie so fast that Algie's head snapped forward.

It was Basement Bart—Mr. Bartholomew, the school caretaker. He was standing in the hall, looking at the two boys, a mop over his shoulder.

"I hate fightin' in the halls," said Basement Bart. "Messy. I don't like messes. Fights should be clean. And short."

"S-short," stammered Algie, staring at the hulking figure of the caretaker. He'd never been that close to Basement Bart before. Basement Bart was huge. Dinosaurian. Megalarge. He was wearing green army camouflage pants tucked into enormous Timberland boots. His faded gray shirt was stretched to ripping over his hulked-out shoulders. Algie couldn't see Basement Bart's eyes because Basement Bart was wearing dark glasses. His gray-streaked hair was pulled into a ponytail at the nape of his neck.

"Yeah." Bart turned his dark glasses in Jason's direction. Jason smiled, trying to look like an all-American boy. "No hair pullin' or any of that sissy stuff."

"Oh. Right!" said Algie enthusiastically. "Well. Are we going to fight, Jason?"

"No," said Jason. He began to back slowly away, keeping his eyes on Basement Bart.

"See ya," said Algie.

Jason took off.

Algie looked at Basement Bart. He smiled.

Basement Bart didn't return the smile. He flipped the mop over his shoulder to the floor. He gave it a little push in Algie's direction.

"He's gonna mop the floor with you, kid," said Bart. Then he smiled.

Algie got one look at Bart's sinister smile and took off, too.

The air had been let out of his bicycle tires at the end of the day. Algie had to walk his bicycle to the service station to put more air in. As he trudged away from Graveyard School, he didn't have to look around to know that Jason was watching and laughing.

"Cheap trick," muttered Algie.

He got a late start on his paper route because of Jason's trick. Even racing through it, he didn't get to Mr. Bates's until almost five o'clock.

Late.

Creepily late.

What would Mr. Bates do? *He's not going to do anything,* Algie reassured himself. *He's probably just some guy who doesn't like for people to bother him. Some weirdo, like a reclusive writer, or something.*

The driveway was endless. The weeds clawed at his pants leg. The tree limbs whipped against his arms.

And it was so dark.

So very dark.

When he reached the end of the driveway, Algie didn't even slow down. He hurled the paper maximum force in the general direction of Mr. Bates's front door. He was already heading back down the driveway when he heard it land on the porch with a thud.

He thought he heard a second thud, the sound of a door being flung open.

But he couldn't be sure. He didn't look back to find out.

Head down, thinking dark, nasty thoughts about Jason Dunnbar, he lurched along Mr. Bates's driveway. He hit Seven Mile Hollow Road at top speed.

He shot through the shadowy tunnel of trees, aiming for the light at the end.

The wheels of his bike sounded like a frightened rodent.

He didn't look up until he almost reached the bridge. He couldn't believe how dark it was getting. It was later than he'd realized.

His parents were going to kill him for riding his bicycle after dark.

Then, as he looked up, he realized it didn't matter. It didn't matter what his parents did to him.

Because he was going to die anyway.

He tried to stop. He tried to scream.

But it was too late.

Straight ahead, by the side of the bridge, the headless ghost of Seven Mile Hollow Road was waiting for Algernon Green.

CHAPTER
8

"Aaaaaaaaaaaah!" screamed Algie.

The ghost was huge. It seemed to float above the ground. It flew toward Algie at top speed.

Algie swerved. He began to pedal as fast as he could.

He felt a swoosh of icy ghost air as the headless apparition reached for him.

Algie didn't dare look. He kept his head down and kept pedaling.

The ghost floated alongside him.

Algie pedaled faster.

The ghost stayed right with him.

They went over the bridge side by side.

And then, suddenly, the ghost wasn't there. The monstrous glowing white thing with no head was gone.

Algie didn't look back to see what had happened to the ghost.

He didn't stop until he reached his house. He threw

his bicycle down on the grass by the garage and raced through the back door into the kitchen.

Slamming the door behind him, he fell against it, trying to catch his breath.

"Algie, is that you?" his father called.

"Uhhhh," groaned Algie.

"Your turn to set the table," his father said.

"Uuuuuh," said Algie.

His teeth were chattering. His palms were wet. He was sweating so hard that drops of perspiration were running down the inside of his glasses.

He'd just been chased by the headless ghost of Seven Mile Hollow Road. Everything people'd said about Mr. Bates was true.

And more. Much more. And much worse.

The ghost was big. And awful. And headless.

And it was also after Algie. Algie alone.

No one else.

Algie knew it for sure. Because the headless ghost had been riding a bicycle.

The headless bicycle rider was after Algie.

"Are you all right, kiddo?" said Algie's father. He forked up another bite of spaghetti. "What's the matter, don't like my cooking?"

"It's fine, Dad," said Algie. "It's always fine."

That was true. When his father cooked, he always made spaghetti. And it was always just fine.

52

But tonight Algie wasn't hungry.

"Do you believe in ghosts?" he asked abruptly.

He was hoping both his parents would just say no. But of course, they didn't.

His mother wrinkled her brow. "I'm not sure," she said.

"I've never seen a ghost," said his father. "I had a friend once who said he had. Imaginative guy, though."

"My great-aunt used to say she'd grown up in a haunted house," added Mrs. Green. "More spaghetti, anyone?"

"No," said Algie glumly. "Thanks anyway."

His parents were such flakes.

Maybe the kids at school would be able to help.

He couldn't have been more wrong.

"You're kidding!" shrieked Stacey. "The headless ghost!"

"Headless bicycle rider, actually," said Algie the next day, standing on the steps before school, trying to keep his voice calm. "You see . . ."

"Was he carrying an ax? Did he try to grab your head?"

"Stacey, will you listen?"

"Park!" Stacey waved at Park. "Guess what happened?"

"They're going to start using designated hitters in the National League," said Park.

"Forget baseball," said Stacey.

A look of outrage crossed Park's face. But before he could say anything, Stacey rushed on. "The headless ghost chased Algie yesterday!"

"What! No way!" Park thumped Algie on the arm as if Algie had accomplished something wonderful.

"It wasn't my idea of a good time," said Algie. "I could have been *killed*."

"Awesome. What did it look like? Was its head all bloody? Was it carrying an ax?"

Algie said, "It was riding a bicycle, okay? And it was enormous, and I didn't see its head. All I saw was this big white headless thing coming at me, and then I took off."

"It chased him all the way down Seven Mile Hollow Road," said Stacey.

"Wow. It must be the ghost of the guy Mr. Bates beheaded." Park stopped. He said thoughtfully, "But why was it riding a bicycle?"

"I don't know. But seeing that thing on a bicycle riding alongside me was even creepier than just seeing it floating along the road," answered Algie.

"What're you going to do? Are you going to quit your paper route? Ax Mr. Bates from your customer list? Ax. Get it? Ax."

"We get it, Park," said Stacey, rolling her eyes. "What are you going to do, Algie?"

"I don't know. I was hoping you'd know what to do," said Algie.

54

"I'll tell you what you need to do," said Kirstin, coming up to the three of them. "Here. I had these made. We can stick them to everything. Especially clocks. I'm gonna try to get the clock in the school lunchroom."

Kirstin handed Algie, Stacey, and Park each a handful of small, square stickers. They were white, and on the front of each one it said, "Time to vote smart. Vote Kirstin."

"Cool," said Park.

"I can put some around when I'm walking dogs," said Stacey.

"Good idea. Maybe you could give some to your paper route customers, Algie," said Kirstin.

"I'm trying to stay alive here," Algie said crossly. He stuffed the stickers in his pack without looking at them. "Could we please stick to the point?"

Kirstin looked at Algie in surprise. "Don't you want me to be elected class president? Don't you want me to beat Jason?"

"Don't you want me to stay alive?" snarled Algie. He didn't even care he was snarling at Kirstin, the coolest girl in the class. He was a desperate man.

"Algie had a bad night," said Park.

"Thanks for noticing," said Algie. He folded his arms and retreated into sulky silence as Park and Stacey filled Kirstin in on Algie's meeting with the headless bicycle rider.

"I don't believe it!" Kirstin exclaimed when they were

55

through. She turned to look at Algie. "It's some kind of joke. Did you see who it was?"

"It didn't have a head. It was hard to see the face," answered Algie, still sulking.

"It was somebody in a white sheet," said Kirstin. "It had to be."

"No it wasn't," Algie said. "I would've known."

But hearing Kirstin's words—words he would have liked his parents to have spoken—Algie suddenly wasn't so sure. What if it was just a trick? What if Mr. Bates was really crazy and had decided to pay Algie back for being late delivering the paper?

Customers were weird. They might always be right, but it didn't mean they couldn't be crazy.

"Algie," said Kirstin, her words an uncanny echo of Algie's thoughts, "it's probably just crazy Mr. Bates. Batso Bates. That's all. Next time what you need to do is—"

"Next time!" Algie couldn't believe his ears.

Kirstin stopped. She stared at Algie. "You're not really afraid of Mr. Bates, are you, Algie?"

Algie looked at Kirstin. He looked at Park. He looked at Stacey.

"Huh," he said. He turned his back on all of them and stomped into the school.

Of course, Jason Dunnbar, presidential candidate, had heard about Algie's being chased by the ghost.

Of course, he made fun of Algie the first chance he got.

"I hear Halloween came early for you, Green," said Jason nastily, dribbling the basketball practically on the toes of Algie's sneakers at recess.

Algie curled his toes under inside his sneakers and answered as calmly as he could, "As a matter of fact, Halloween *just* got here."

He stared at Jason, trying to make his eyes look menacing behind his glasses.

Jason glared back. He stopped bouncing the ball. He smiled his all-American kid smile.

Does everyone at Graveyard School have special creepy smiles? wondered Algie. *Do they save them just for me?*

At the sight of Jason's smile, Algie was barely able to keep from shuddering.

"Funny, Algernon. Very funny. Why don't you try that joke on your ghost—right before it tears your head off?" Jason spun and dribbled away. He faked left, then looped a long perfect shot into the net.

"Way to go!" someone shouted, and Jason was back in the recess basketball game.

Kirstin was practicing soccer. Across the playground he could see Maria and Stacey talking under a tree. Park was trying to organize a baseball game.

It was chaos. It seemed so normal.

I'm being chased by a ghost! Algie wanted to scream. *I'm going to be killed!*

57

Doesn't anybody care?

But he knew the answer. Some people thought it was cool. Some people didn't believe it was real. And almost everybody took it in stride.

What kind of school was Graveyard School anyway?

CHAPTER
9

It was because I *was late,* thought Algie suddenly.

Squeak squeak squeak.

The squeak wasn't as bad as it had been. Algie had oiled every single moving part of his bicycle that he could find. One of those parts was the squeaky part. If only he could figure out which one.

But he didn't have time for that.

He'd been late. That was when the ghost—or Mr. Bates in a very real-looking ghost suit—had come after him.

That had to be it. Of course. Mystery solved. Case closed.

Algie threw a paper overhand. If it had been a basketball, it would have stripped the net as it landed exactly on someone's front doormat without even rebounding off the front door.

"I'm good," said Algie aloud.

Kirstin *was* right. Batso Bates. Had to be.

So what would he do when—no, if he saw Mr. Bates again? Pull his bike over and grab Mr. Bates by the sheet and give him a good talking-to? Apologize for being late and promise it would never happen again? Tell Mr. Bates the customer was always right, but please to stop with the ghost joke?

Was this Mr. Bates's idea of a joke? A good time?

Algie turned his bicycle toward Seven Mile Hollow Road. He pumped up to cruising speed and thought about it. He wondered what kind of person Mr. Bates really was.

Maybe he wasn't really an ax killer. Maybe he was just a retired ax salesman. Maybe someone had asked him, "So what do you do, Mr. Bates?" and had misunderstood the answer, and that was how the rumor had gotten started.

The sight of the bridge made Algie pause. But it looked peaceful in the late-afternoon light. Quaint. Charming. All those words his mother used when they went on vacation.

Nothing had changed along the Bates driveway. The house still stood, sagging and abandoned-looking. Algie threw the paper up on the porch and turned without waiting to see it land, just as he always did.

He didn't even need to look closely at where he was aiming anymore. It was true of all his customers. Once he had a fix on the target, he could nail it with just a quick glance in that direction.

Yes. He was definitely gonna go out for baseball next year. And if Park was the pitcher, he'd better watch out.

See, I'm not scared, Algie told himself, pedaling back down the driveway. *I can think of all kinds of things calmly. I'm not even thinking about some weirdo in a ghost outfit.*

But when he reached Seven Mile Hollow Road, he felt his heart start to pound.

Nothing wrong with being prepared, he told himself. He closed the gate to Mr. Bates's driveway slowly. He got on his bike and headed toward the bridge. Quaint. Charming.

He tried to ignore how dark it suddenly seemed to be.

As he got to the bridge, he kept his head up. He looked from left to right, determined not to be caught by surprise when—

"Give me your head . . . " it moaned, almost in his ear.

Algie was prepared.

He screamed even louder than he had the day before. He began to pedal his bike at hyperspeed. If his bike had been a spaceship, he would have warped out.

This time the ghost wasn't wearing a sheet. It had on a suit. A loose, flapping suit that had a neon glow to it.

It was an ugly suit. It would have been an ugly suit in any circumstances.

But this suit was really ugly. Because where the head

61

was supposed to emerge from the collar and tie was nothing at all.

Unless you counted the red ring around the collar.

Algie didn't take the time to look closely. He pedaled faster.

And the ghost pedaled right behind him. But while Algie's bike squeaked and moaned and clattered, the ghost's bike didn't make any sound at all.

"Give me your headddddd," the ghost moaned again as Algie shot over the bridge.

Algie didn't answer. He didn't answer and he didn't look back and he didn't stop until he got all the way home.

"I'm going with you."

"What? What makes you think I'm going back?"

"Don't be silly," said Kirstin. "Of course, you're going back. And I'm going with you."

"Why?" asked Algie. He was standing by his bicycle. The sun was shining. The birds were singing. And his heart was pounding with fear. Because school was over again for the day and it was time to start his paper route.

Everyone had thought his story was cool. Everyone had lots of theories about ax murderers and ghosts. Polly Hannah had kept talking about chain saw massacres.

None of them had helped Algie out.

The only good part was that Jason hadn't even come

near Algie all day. He'd been too busy campaigning. The election was only two days away.

"Why?" repeated Algie.

Kirstin shrugged. "Why not? Besides, you're supposed to be my campaign manager. But I don't think you're giving my campaign your complete attention. Once we've taken care of this problem, you'll be able to concentrate on the important stuff."

"Oh," said Algie feebly. Was everybody crazy? he wondered. Even Kirstin?

Or was it just him? Was he crazy and everyone else at Graveyard School normal?

He wondered how he would break the news to his parents. *Time to move again, Mom and Dad. Everyone at my school is nuts.*

Somehow he didn't think it would work.

Kirstin was staring at Algie. He realized that he was supposed to say something else besides "oh."

"Oh," he said again. "Okay. Well . . . I'll deliver my other papers and then meet you at the corner of Grove Hill Road and Seven Mile Hollow at—at four-fifteen."

"Got it." Kirstin slung her pack over her shoulder and walked briskly off to join her girlfriends and walk home.

Algie got on his bike and went to pick up his newspapers to do his paper route.

He made several bad throws that day. Twice he had to get off his bike, go get a newspaper, and put it up on the porch because he'd missed completely.

Maybe he wouldn't be pitching for the baseball team next year. Maybe he was the kind that cracked under pressure.

Of course, if he died of fright before then, it wouldn't be a problem anyway.

Kirstin wasn't at the intersection of Seven Mile Hollow and Grove Hill Road when he got there. Algie slowed down and looked around. He didn't see her anywhere. With a sigh he pulled off the road and sat down under a tree.

The golden sunlight of late afternoon filtered through the branches. A squirrel ran up a tree and scolded him from the safety of the branches just out of reach. Birds sang.

It was a peaceful, pleasant afternoon. Unless you were on your way to meet a ghost.

Algie looked at his watch. He stood up. He paced nervously up and down.

No Kirstin.

Had she forgotten? Had she gotten lost? Had she misunderstood him?

Had it been some kind of cruel joke?

Time was flying. And he wasn't having fun. With one last look up and down Grove Hill Road, Algie got on his bike reluctantly and began to pedal down Seven Mile Hollow. He kept looking over his shoulder, hoping he'd see Kirstin, riding her bike at top speed and shouting, "Wait for me! Sorry I was late!"

But no Kirstin appeared. No human being at all appeared. Just the usual collection of farms. Then fields. Then overgrown pastures being gradually eaten by the woods.

And now he was late. Again.

"Just ahead," he said aloud, pretending he was a sports announcer, "is the famous Ghost Bridge. World champion pitcher and cyclist Algernon Green has been known to go over that bridge at speeds in excess of— of—twenty miles an hour."

He didn't slow down on the bridge. He left Mr. Bates's gate open so he could make a quick exit. He tore down the endless driveway and hurled the paper from the very edge of the clearing in which the house sat.

And he didn't even wait to see it land.

When he got back to Mr. Bates's gate, he slammed it shut and leaped on his bike as if gate slamming and bike remounting were Olympic events and he were going for the gold medal.

He went down Seven Mile Hollow as fast as he could go. He'd almost reached the bridge when disaster struck.

The chain came off his bicycle and got completely tangled in the gears.

"No! No, no, no, no!" screamed Algie. He pulled his bike to one side. He tried to jerk the chain free. All he got was a lot of disgusting grease on his hands. He wiped his hands on his jeans and turned the bike over.

He looked at his watch. He wasn't surprised at how dark it was getting. He could see how late it was.

Quickly he looked up and down Seven Mile Hollow. No one. Just the last light of day poking little fingers of yellow through the trees.

Algie groaned. He bent down and jerked at the chain again.

It was totally stuck.

As fast as he could he began to work the chain free. But it was hard to go as fast as he wanted because he had to keep straightening up and looking over his shoulder.

What would he do if he saw anybody?

What would he do if he saw the ghost?

Throw his newspaper pack at it? Try to outrun it on foot? Tell it to mind its own business and go haunt someone with a working bicycle and a fair chance of getting away?

Get beheaded?

Algie gulped. He bent back over the chain. He wiped his hands on his jeans and gave the chain one last jerk.

It pulled free. Carefully Algie put the chain back on the gearwheel. Carefully he turned his bike upright.

Then he got back on and rode as fast as he could for the bridge.

It was almost dark now, later than it had ever been.

He rode up on the bridge, forcing himself to ignore the

hollow sound of the boards, forcing himself to ignore the drop beneath his feet.

Forcing himself not to look for the ghost.

Just a little ways to go, he told himself. *No problem. You can do it.*

There is no ghost.

It's just Old Man Bates in a ghost outfit. And you can outrun him.

He'd made it. He was over the bridge. Just ahead was the edge of the first little farm on Seven Mile Hollow. He'd made it.

He was safe.

And then the ghost stepped out into the middle of the road.

CHAPTER
10

"Aaaaaaaaaaahhhh!" Algie screamed. He braked so hard he fell over.

The ghost grabbed him by the arm.

Algie closed his eyes and hit the ghost as hard as he could.

"Ow! Hey, chill," said the ghost.

Algie opened his eyes. "Kirstin?"

"Who did you think it was?"

"The ghost," said Algie crossly. He got up and inspected himself for damage.

"I'm sorry I was late," said Kirstin. "So is this where you saw the alleged ghost?"

"Alleged?"

"I don't think it was a real ghost you saw."

"Okay. I saw the *alleged* ghost back at the bridge." Algie pointed in the direction from which he had just come.

"Right. Let's go." Kirstin walked over to her bike and got on it.

"Are you *serious*? Do you know how late it is?"

"This will just take a few minutes, Algie. And I brought a flashlight. One of those big ones." Kirstin took off.

Algie watched her pedal away. Then he realized that if he didn't go with her, he was going to be left standing alone on Seven Mile Hollow.

"Hey! Wait for me!" he called. He caught up with Kirstin just as they reached the bridge.

"This is where it happened?" asked Kirstin.

"Uh-huh," said Algie. He swallowed hard.

Kirstin braked and got off her bike, leaning it against a tree.

Algie stopped, too. "What're you doing?"

"Looking for clues," said Kirstin.

"Right . . . ghost footprints." Algie got off his bike reluctantly and propped it next to Kirstin's.

Kirstin came back toward Algie and got down and studied the front wheels of both bikes. "Not ghost footprints," she said. "Bike tracks. Look at the patterns on yours and mine. Then look at the patterns of the bike tracks in the road. If it's a different pattern, then it's a different bike. And if there is another bike tire pattern, it means that the ghost was riding a real bicycle."

"So?"

"So why would a ghost do that? I mean, if a ghost is

70

on a bicycle, why wouldn't it use a ghost bicycle? One that doesn't leave tracks at all."

Algie had to admit it. He was impressed. He bent down and checked out the tires on his bicycle and Kirstin's.

"Let's split up and check around," he said.

The two of them walked up and down the road. They checked the bridge. They looked behind trees and rocks and under fallen logs.

"It's getting really late," said Algie at last. He tried not to sound worried.

"I don't think he's gonna show up," said Kirstin. "I think he's not going to bother you when you're not alone."

"Great. So what am I supposed to do, hire a body-guard to deliver Mr. Bates's paper?"

Kirstin started making her way back toward the bicycles. At the middle of the bridge she stopped and peered over the side.

"Nothing's down there," said Algie, trying not to look.

"Mmm," said Kirstin. "The sides down the creek are pretty steep, too. I guess you couldn't get a bike down there."

"Unless you were a ghost. *And* your bike didn't leave any tire tracks."

"Algie, do you really believe you saw a ghost?"

Algie got on his bike and turned to Kirstin. "I don't know. But if it wasn't a ghost, who was it?"

• • •

"Hey, it's the ghostbusters," said Jason.

"That's Ms. Ghostbuster to you, Jason," said Kirstin, walking past him. Algie didn't say anything. He stopped at his locker and got out his books.

"Oooooh, Algie, I'm going to cut off your head," said Jason.

"Shut up," muttered Algie. But he didn't mutter it loud enough for Jason to hear him.

"Did Kirstin save you from the big mean headless bicycle rider?"

Jason and his friends cracked up.

Algie ignored them.

If people make fun of you and you ignore them, his father always said, they'll stop. Just don't let them know it bothers you.

Clearly, thought Algie, ignoring Jason in math class, *my father was never a kid.*

"What happens if Algie washes his neck?" asked Jason loudly in the lunchroom as Algie walked by.

"What?" asked Ken Dahl.

"His head falls off!" Jason laughed. The whole table laughed.

Possibly the whole lunchroom laughed. Algie wasn't sure. He was busy ignoring everybody.

He sat down with Park. Park had a big grin on his face.

"What're *you* smiling at?" asked Algie.

Park wiped the grin off his face. "Nothing. Are you gonna deliver papers today?"

"Yes," said Algie.

Park waited. Algie started eating his lunch.

Park tried again. "You didn't see anything yesterday? You and Kirstin?"

"No."

"You know what's weird," said Park. "What's weird is that the ghost changed clothes. I mean, the first time you saw it, it was all white and floaty, like a kid's ghost Halloween costume, right?"

"Mmm," said Algie.

"And the second time you said it was wearing this sort of glow-in-the-dark suit, right?"

"Right."

"I never heard of ghosts that changed clothes. I mean, I thought they always had to wear what they were wearing when they, you know, departed this world."

"If you can rise out your grave to haunt someone, I guess you can wear what you want," said Algie.

"True," said Park.

Algie looked across the lunchroom. Jason had pulled his shirt up over his head. He was walking around with his arms stuck out. "Wherrre's mmmmmyyyyy headdddd?" he called loudly.

"I'm glad the election is tomorrow," said Algie. "I can hardly wait to vote against Jason."

In study hall Algie wrote Mr. Korman Bates a note:

73

DEAR MR. BATES,

I can't deliver the afternoon newspaper to you anymore. I will return the money I owe you to you separately, but I wanted to let you know so you could make arrangements for someone else to deliver your paper as soon as possible.

Sincerely,
ALGERNON GREEN

He reread the letter. He liked the sound of it. Very professional, he decided.

And mailing it right after school, so Mr. Bates would get it right away, would be the professional thing to do, too, he decided.

The clerk at the post office sold him a prestamped envelope.

"Could I have a receipt?" asked Algie.

"A receipt?" she asked. "For one stamped envelope."

"It's a business expense," explained Algie.

"A business expense," the clerk said. "Sure." She gave him a receipt. Algie stuffed it in his pocket and went over to a counter to address the envelope.

But then he stopped. Did he just put Seven Mile Hollow Road? Was he supposed to write a house number? He didn't think Mr. Bates had one. Maybe it was a box number. Or maybe Mr. Bates had a post office box right there in the post office. And what about the zip code? Was it the same?

He'd thrown away the envelope that the letter had come in long ago. And he couldn't remember the exact address.

Holding the half-addressed envelope, he went back over to the window.

The clerk looked sourly down at him. "Yes?"

"I'd like to check on an address."

"We don't give out addresses," said the clerk. She folded her hands in front of her and looked over Algie's head.

"What about zip codes?" said Algie. "Do you give out zip codes? Can you tell me if I have the right zip code?"

The clerk sighed. She rolled her eyes. She got up in super slow motion and trudged over to a big book at the back of the post office.

"What's the address?" she bellowed.

"I don't know," said Algie.

The back door of the post office opened, and a letter carrier came in. "Done for the day, Gladys," he said cheerfully.

"Hooray for you, Marty," the clerk answered sarcastically. To Algie she said, "If you don't know the address, how can I give you the zip code?"

Algie sighed. "Look. All I know is that Mr. Bates lives at the very end of Seven Mile Hollow Road."

Marty looked up. He stared at Algie. He frowned. "Mr. Bates? Seven Mile Hollow Road?"

"Mr. Korman Bates. He's a customer of mine. I deliver the afternoon newspaper to him. He, ah, used to own a motel," said Algie. He was going to explain more, but the funny expression on the letter carrier's face stopped him.

"At the end of Seven Mile Hollow?" asked Marty, the letter carrier.

"Zip code is the same for all of Grove Hill," said Gladys. She slammed the book shut. "Why didn't you tell me it was here in Grove Hill?"

Algie said to Marty, "You know Mr. Bates? If I just put his name and that he lives at the end of Seven Mile Hollow Road, will the letter get to him?"

Marty shook his head slowly.

"So what am I going to do? Deliver it myself?"

After pushing his cap back, Marty scratched his head. He appeared to be thinking hard. At last he said, "No. No, I don't think that would work either, son."

Algie wanted to scream. He wanted to pound the counter with his fists. He wanted to pound Gladys and Marty and all the packages that said "Fragile/Handle with Care." *"Why not?"* he said. He stopped. He took a deep breath. "Why not?"

"Because," said Marty. "Because no Mr. Bates lives

out on Seven Mile Hollow. In fact, I don't think anyone named Korman Bates lives in Grove Hill, and I ought to know. I've been a letter carrier for thirty years. Walked every route in town."

Gladys said, with sour satisfaction, "Then you don't need a zip code at all."

"What?" Algie couldn't believe his ears. "This is some kind of joke, right?"

Marty gave Algie a reproachful look. "Son, I represent the United States government. I wouldn't joke."

"Are you sure?" asked Algie. "You're sure no one named Korman Bates lives in Grove Hill? No one named Korman Bates lives out on Seven Mile Hollow Road?"

"Sure I'm sure. That road . . ." Marty paused and shook his head. "Bad news. Anyway, the old house at the end of it used to be the old Bates place. No one's lived there for years, though. The last of the Bates family, brothers they were, they're long gone. One came to a bad end, had an accident chopping wood . . . buried the poor guy with his ax. The other one, he left and went to work for one of those big fancy hotel chains. Why, there hasn't been a Bates in this part of the country for years."

CHAPTER
11

Algie walked home in a daze. If Mr. Bates didn't exist, then who had hired him to deliver the newspapers? Who had paid him? In cash? And why?

He delivered his papers mechanically. He got no joy in his sliders, his fast pitches to the front doormats that he imagined were home plate. After he'd delivered his last paper, he went slowly home.

He ate dinner without speaking. He did his homework without complaining. He went to bed early.

Maybe people had once known the true story of the Bates brothers years before. But somehow the story had gotten twisted around. Now everyone believed that an ax murderer named Korman Bates lived out at the end of Seven Mile Hollow Road.

But it wasn't true. The house to which Algie had been delivering papers was empty. Abandoned. Deserted. And if Mr. Bates didn't exist, neither did the headless ghost.

Why hadn't he noticed that the house was empty? Why had he believed what everyone else had told him?

He thought about opening the envelope. He remembered the cash falling out in his hand. He could almost hear his father saying, "No such thing as easy money, Algernon." And his mother adding, "Everything has its price."

Tomorrow, Algie decided, he was going to take a close look at the old Bates place.

Squeak, squeak, grinddddd . . .

The chain had come off his bike again. Algie sighed. He was turning into the bad-luck kid. He got off his bike to wrestle the chain back into place.

He remembered the last time that had happened, how freaked out he'd been. How he'd expected a headless ghost to come sneaking up behind him and behead him with one swoop of its ghostly ax.

At least the chain wasn't as tangled up in the gear-wheels as it had been. Algie gave it a final tug and poke and got back on his bike.

He realized that it had gotten dark. Very dark.

And he hadn't even reached the end of Seven Mile Hollow Road. He was going to have to hurry to get to the Bates place and back before nightfall. Now that he knew the ghost didn't exist, he'd gone back to worrying about his parents' grounding him for life for getting home late.

Good old parents.

He reached the bridge. He was halfway over when the thing came out from the other side and rode onto the bridge.

"Algggieeee," it said.

"I'm not afraid of you," said Algie. But he stopped his bike.

The ghost kept riding toward him. It was wearing a suit again. *Some stupid Halloween costume,* Algie thought.

The ghost rode closer. It raised its arm.

It was holding an ax.

Algie's courage left him. He turned his bike around and began to ride back along Seven Mile Hollow as fast as he could.

"I want your headdddddd," moaned the ghost.

"You're no ghost!" gasped Algie. "I know who you are!"

"Algggieeee."

"Because how would you know my name?"

Algie heard a horrible crunching sound. His bike swerved dangerously. He looked over his shoulder.

The ghost had swung the ax at Algie and missed. Now half of Algie's rear fender was twisted off from the blow.

"Algie . . . " said the ghost. It left the bicycle and floated alongside Algie. Behind Algie, the bike kept on rolling forward. It bumped against Algie's rear wheel.

Algie's blood ran cold. "No," he gasped.

"Algie," said the ghost. The bloody collar seemed to

turn in Algie's direction. The ghostly glow seemed to fill the air. Slowly the ghost raised the eerily gleaming ax.

"I want your headddd," moaned the ghost, and brought the ax down.

"Noooooo!" Algie sat up. He put both hands to his throat. His head was still firmly attached. He was sitting in his bed in his own room.

It had been a bad dream.

There was no ghost.

"There is no ghost," Algie said aloud, just to make sure.

No one answered him. No one argued with him.

Gradually his heart stopped pounding. He lay back down. He thought about the dream.

In the dream the ghost had been real. In the dream the ghost had used his name.

But in the dream he'd known who the ghost was.

And he knew who the ghost was now.

He knew who the ghost was. And he knew what he was going to do.

Algie smiled in the darkness. He couldn't see himself smile, but if he had, he would have realized something.

He'd officially become a part of Graveyard School. He'd perfected the evil Graveyard School smile.

And it was truly terrifying.

• • •

"Don't forget to vote," said Kirstin. She was standing at the top of the stairs, handing out pencils that said "I voted smart. I voted Kirstin."

Everyone was grabbing for them. "Great idea," someone said.

"My campaign manager thought of it," said Kirstin. She looked over at Algie and smiled.

The smile didn't bother Algie anymore. He just smiled back and kept passing out pencils.

"But I can't vote for her," a first grader said, looking worried.

Kirstin overheard and said, "Keep the pencil. Remember to vote for me when I run for governor. And president of the country."

"Cool," said the kid, stashing the pencil in his back pocket and taking off.

The stream of kids began to thin out.

Jason came up the steps. He saw Kirstin and glared.

She smiled.

Jason switched his glare to Algie.

Algie smiled, too.

Leaning so close to Algie that they were almost forehead to forehead, Jason said, "You're a loser, Green. You know that."

"I don't think so," said Algie. "Want a pencil, Dunnbar? It's not too late to vote smart."

"I'm not through with you yet," Jason snarled. He grabbed the pencil out of Algie's hand and snapped it in two and threw it at Algie's feet. He shoved Algie to one side, hard, and lunged up the stairs and through the door of the school.

Algie kept the smile on his face. He wasn't afraid of Jason anymore.

And if Jason wasn't through with Algie, well, it was Jason who was going to be sorry . . .

After a long, boring speech about politics and government in homeroom and another long, boring announcement by Mr. Lucre about being responsible students and choosing the best representative for each class, the students in every class were given ballots for their class.

Algie voted smart. He voted for Kirstin. When he'd taken his ballot up front and stuffed it into the ballot box, he looked across the room and gave Kirstin the thumbs-up sign.

She grinned back—a nice, normal smile.

In the back of the room Jason scowled. But Algie didn't even notice.

Dr. Morthouse called a special assembly at the end of the day to announce the election results. Just as they had on the front steps, the students filed into the auditorium and seated themselves in order, first graders in front, second graders next, then third, fourth, fifth, and finally sixth graders in the back. Algie found a seat next to Park.

"How's the ghost job going?" asked Park sympathetically.

"I'm, ah, canceling Mr. Bates," said Algie.

Kirstin slid in next to Algie. "You're giving up your paper route?" she asked in surprise.

"Just Mr. Bates," said Algie.

"You're letting a fake ghost scare you away?"

"Quiet, please," Dr. Morthouse said into the microphone. She smiled out at the students, and something shiny glinted in her mouth.

The noise in the auditorium began to die down.

"No!" Algie lowered his voice. "But I've got a plan. A plan to make the ghost go away." He turned toward Kirstin so Park couldn't hear what he was saying. Looking deep into Kirstin's eyes, Algie said, "I'm going to take that ghost out this afternoon."

Kirstin's mouth dropped open. "You are? Wow. Want some help?"

"Thank you, I can do it myself," said Algie.

"Students," said Dr. Morthouse. She gave the packed auditorium the old school smile.

Silence fell instantly.

"Goooood," said Dr. Morthouse. "We now have the results of our class elections. To all the students who ran for office, my congratulations. Participation in government at any level is the mark of a good citizen. The student officials of today are the leaders of tomorrow."

"Now I'm really worried," muttered Park.

The principal began to read out the names. One by one the class officers were announced and made to go up to the stage to say a word of thanks into the microphone and then to stand in a line between Dr. Morthouse and Mr. Lucre. When they reached the sixth grade, Dr. Morthouse went through all the other officers, saving class president for last. Then she paused.

"The sixth grade had an unusually close race this year," she said. "I'd like to congratulate the winner and say here that I hope both candidates will work together for the good of the sixth grade and of Grove Hill School."

"I won," said Kirstin firmly.

"The new sixth-grade class president is . . . Kirstin Bjorg."

Kirstin jumped up as the class began to applaud. Several of the kids in the lower classes started waving their pencils in the air.

Kirstin's acceptance speech was brief and characteristically self-confident. "Thanks to all you sixth graders who decided to vote smart. I especially want to thank my campaign manager, Algernon Green, who came up with some great campaign ideas—"

Park dug his elbow approvingly into Algie's side. Several people turned to look in Algie's direction and nod. Algie felt an unexpected thrill at Kirstin's words.

"—and I want you all to know that I'm gonna do a great job."

Shouts of approval rang out as Kirstin flashed victory

signs and Dr. Morthouse hastily reclaimed the microphone.

Several people congratulated Algie as he made his way through the assembly-happy crowd of students Dr. Morthouse dismissed from the auditorium. He thanked them all modestly. He wished he could stay and enjoy the victory.

But he still had a job to do.

Kirstin caught up with him as he was unlocking his bike outside the school. "Algernon."

Algie jumped. "What! Why'd you call me that?"

"Because this is official. I just want you to know that I really appreciate your help and all your super campaign ideas. I know Jason is still giving you grief, and as class president I'm going to give the matter my full attention. When I'm through, Jason will never bother you again."

"Thanks," said Algie. He looked around. Jason was standing on the steps of the school. Algie could practically hear Jason grinding his teeth in rage.

Algie grinned. He raised his hand and waved at Jason.

Looking in the direction Algie was waving, Kirstin lifted her chin. "I'll take care of him. Trust me."

"Thanks, Kirstin," Algie said loudly. "I'm glad I could help. Well, I've got to go deliver the papers. I don't want to get to Mr. Bates's place too late."

Jason folded his arms across his chest and watched as Algie rode away.

Kirstin wouldn't be able to do much of anything about

Jason, thought Algie. Not even if she was class president *and* the most popular girl in the class. But it was nice of her to offer to help. Thanks to Kirstin, he didn't feel like such an outsider at the new school.

In fact, Graveyard School felt just like home. He hoped his parents would decide to stay for a while.

And he didn't need any help with Jason now. He'd had all he was going to take. Like Superman coming out of a phone booth, Algernon Green was about to lose his meek, mild self.

Jason wasn't going to know what hit him.

CHAPTER

12

Algie rode slowly up to the house. To his right the tattered, ancient scarecrow's clothes fluttered in a faint breeze. At the foot of the front steps Algie stopped.

He checked it out. Boarded-over windows. Ancient rotting curtains behind the watery panes of old glass in the windows that weren't boarded over. Sagging shutters and missing boards and a roof that was just this side of caving in completely.

And the big black door had a big black board nailed completely across it. The front door of the old Bates place hadn't been opened in years.

Algie grinned. What a sucker he'd been.

But he wasn't a sucker anymore. He got on his bike and headed back down the overgrown driveway. He wanted to make sure he got where he was going in plenty of time.

He'd never arrived at the old bridge so early. He pulled his bike to one side and hid it in the bushes facing outward. He checked the chain and made sure everything was working right. He practiced getting on in a hurry and riding out into the road and onto the bridge. He practiced taking his hands off the wheel as he rode up onto the bridge.

Then he opened his backpack. He took out his Frankenstein suit with the rubber hands from Halloween the year before. He took out the moon white hockey mask he'd bought at costume store. When it was exposed to enough light, it would glow in the dark with an eerie greenish glow. Algie hung the mask up on a low branch in the sun to make sure it would glow good and bright when the dark came.

He changed clothes. He sat down by his bike to wait.

The sunlight gradually faded. The shadows grew deeper beneath the trees. Algie stood up and shifted the mask so it would catch the last bit of sun. He got on his bike just to be ready.

A few minutes later, as the sun started to disappear into the trees, Algie heard the sound of someone coming up the road.

Algie peered out.

The headless bicycle rider was coming down Seven Mile Hollow Road.

At the far side of the bridge the ghost stopped. It rode slowly up onto the bridge and stopped at the top of it. It peered down the road toward the Bates place.

Quickly Algie drew back into the shadows of the trees. He reached quietly up and took the mask down and pulled it over his head. He crouched low over the handlebars of his bike.

"C'mon, c'mon, *come on*," Algie whispered to himself.

The ghost hesitated at the top of the bridge a moment longer. Was it suspicious? Did it sense that Algernon Green, ghostbuster, was waiting for it on the other side?

Algie held his breath. At last the ghost put its feet back on the pedals and coasted down the other side of the bridge.

Just as it reached the bottom, Algie shot out of the dark shadows of the trees and into the road. He twisted the front wheel of his bike sideways and headed straight for the ghost.

"Ooooooh," wailed Algie. "Give me your headddd!"

The ghost screamed the loudest scream Algie had ever heard in his life. It braked and turned its bike sideways. It fell off and then scrambled to its hands and knees and jumped back on.

"Who's got my head?" moaned Algie.

"Aaaaaaaaaah." The ghost turned its bike around and fled.

Algie couldn't help himself. He'd meant to follow the ghost. He'd meant to really make it suffer.

But he started laughing.

The ghost stopped halfway up the bridge. It looked over its shoulder. It got off its bike and dropped it with a menacing clatter and began to walk back down the bridge toward Algie.

"Ha-ha, ha-ha," Algie gasped. "That was the funniest thing I've ever seen. I wish *you* could have seen your face, Jason."

Jason, wearing what looked like an old tuxedo complete with cape and padded shoulders and a high white collar with red painted around it, kept stalking toward Algie.

Algie kept laughing. He couldn't stop.

"You thought that was funny? I'll show you funny," growled Jason.

Algie pushed his mask back. He laughed harder.

Jason stopped. "You jerk."

Trying to stop laughing and get his breath back, Algie nodded. "B-but you started it."

"So what if I did?" said Jason. "I oughta kill you."

"Jason. Be fair. I just did to you what you did to me."

Jason kept glaring at Algie. "And your costume isn't even as good as mine," he said.

"True," said Algie. "But it's the best I could come up with on such short notice. You had more time to plan yours. It's a great outfit, too. I mean, it fooled me."

Jason looked sort of pleased. "You think so? It's my old Dracula costume. I padded the shoulders and turned the collar of the shirt up high."

"How could you see?"

"I cut two holes right below the neck, see? When I pulled the collar up, the padded shoulders were on each side of my ears."

Jason was no dummy, thought Algie. He wondered if he would have figured it out if Jason hadn't scared him so badly the first time he showed up.

"How come you used a sheet the first time?" asked Algie.

"I didn't think you'd be so scared. But when I heard you were, and how you were telling everybody about the headless bicycle rider, I decided to go for it. That's when I remembered the Dracula gear."

"Decent," said Algie.

Jason almost smiled. Then he seemed to realize whom he was talking to.

"You little creep. It's your fault I lost that election."

Uh-oh, thought Algie. He'd forgotten about that. He'd been so intent on paying Jason back that he'd completely forgotten.

Quickly he said, "One thing I don't get, though. How did you get the money to pay me in advance to deliver all those papers to the old Bates place?"

"What are you talking about?" asked Jason suspiciously.

"I got that note asking me to deliver the papers and you paid me in advance—"

"I didn't send you any note. I just heard you were sup-

93

posed to be delivering the paper to Old Man Bates."

"But there is no Old Man Bates."

Jason looked even more puzzled and suspicious. "Yes, there is," he said. "And you couldn't *pay* me to go anywhere near that place. I'm not a chicken, but I'm not stupid either."

"But no one lives in the old Bates place," said Algie.

"Says who?" asked Jason. "Listen, you can believe what you want. But I know what I know."

Algie stared at Jason.

Jason stared at Algie.

Then Algie said, "There weren't any newspapers on the porch this afternoon when I went and checked. The place is empty. Deserted. Abandoned. And I've been delivering papers for weeks now. You didn't go and get them to make it look like someone lived there?"

"No way," said Jason. "And I wouldn't send you money to deliver a paper there either. I'd just send you a note and tell you I'd pay later. *I* know how paper routes work . . . I wish I'd thought of sending you that note, though."

"But if you didn't send me the note, who did?"

"Mr. Bates," said Jason. He stepped a little closer to Algie. His voice got menacing again. "Now, Algernon—"

A sound stopped them.

A faint sound.

A weird sound.

Algie looked nervously around. "Didja hear that?"

"I didn't hear anything," snapped Jason. But he looked over his shoulder, too.

"It's getting sort of late and dark," said Algie. "Maybe we could . . . "

His voice trailed off. Jason was looking past Algie's shoulder, his eyes wide with terror, his face pale.

"I'm not falling for another one of your stupid tricks, Jason," said Algie.

Jason's mouth opened. His lips moved. But no sound came out. He began to back away from Algie.

"Jason," said Algie. "Quit that!"

Jason raised his arm and pointed a trembling finger.

Algie felt a faint coolness blow past him. The hair on his neck stood up. The hair on his arms stood up. Goose bumps crawled up his spine.

Slowly he turned.

A ghost stood at the foot of the bridge.

A real ghost.

It was dressed in ordinary clothes. That was one of the things that was so scary about it: the ordinary clothes. But somehow the ghost's clothes made the costumes Algie and Jason were wearing look silly.

For one thing, it had an unearthly glow about it. For another, the ghost had on a funny-looking backpack, a strangely bulging backpack.

And worst of all, it held on to a helmet, which must

have contained the ghost's head. It was hovering, bicycle and all, nearly a foot above the ground. The whole apparition rippled and wavered against the gathering darkness behind it. It didn't make a sound. But icy coldness seemed to be spreading out in a pool around it.

And all around them the woods had grown strangely silent.

Then it spoke. "Do you have my head?"

The sound was low and mournful. It was colder than ice and as empty as death. And it wasn't human.

Algie backed up so fast he bumped into Jason and almost dropped his own bicycle. "Uh—n-n-no. Uh, no, sir."

Keeping his eyes on the ghastly floating headless thing, Algie groped for his bicycle and wrestled it upright.

"I'm getting out of here!" Jason screamed.

"Wait for meeeee!" screamed Algie.

Almost at the same time the two boys jerked their bikes around and jumped on and began to pedal for their lives.

"Wait for mmmmmmmmemmmmmeeeeee," echoed the ghost, and slowly, almost casually, it rose above the bridge and floated over.

"*Aaahhhhhhhh,*" screamed Algie.

"*Aahhhhhhhhhhh,*" screamed Jason.

"Come bacccck," moaned the ghost. Its voice faded slightly.

Algie looked back.

The ghost had stopped at the bend in the road. It hovered there, glowing, horrible, headless above the ground.

And then it began to laugh.

The laugh was even more horrible than the voice. But the worst thing of all, Algie realized, as he pedaled around the curve and out of sight of the ghost and into sight of the first farm on Seven Mile Hollow on the way back to Grove Hill Road, wasn't the laugh.

The worst thing of all was that the sound of the ghost's voice, the sound of its laughter were coming from inside the backpack. The head wasn't in the helmet after all.

The two boys didn't stop until they reached their neighborhood. Then, gasping, panting, choking, Jason wheeled his bike to a stop by the curb.

"I didn't see it," he said hoarsely.

"I did," said Algie.

He and Jason looked at each other. Then Jason said, "Just don't mess with me again, okay, Green?"

He got on his bike and rode away.

Algie watched until Jason was out of sight. Then he realized he was standing all alone on the street. And that it was dark. And that his parents were going to kill him for being late.

He wondered what he was going to do with the money for delivering the papers to the Bates place. He decided he'd mail it after all. He just wouldn't put a return address on it.

At least he would have tried.

He headed home, too.

Back on Seven Mile Hollow Road the ghost stood for a long time in the gathering gloom. Then it turned and began to ride back along the road. A sickly green gleam caught the ghost's attention. It bent and picked up the glow-in-the-dark hockey mask.

"Interesting," murmured the ghost in its dead voice.

It hung the mask on a tree and kept going, the wheels of its ghost bike making no sound high above the road. It floated over the bridge and stopped on the other side, where Algie had left his backpack and his clothes. The ghost picked up the backpack and opened it. A spare newspaper was inside. The ghost took it out, zipped the pack up, and hung it up on a tree where it could be seen from the road.

Then the ghost opened its own backpack. It took out a head and settled it neatly and without fuss on its own neck and shoulders.

Kirstin massaged the side of her neck and twisted her head a few times to make sure everything was working right. Then she put the helmet on. She laughed softly. Humans were so weird. And they were scared of the strangest things. Maybe that's why she liked hanging out with them.

Still laughing, Kirstin stuck the newspaper in her backpack and zipped it up. Then she slung the pack over her shoulder, got back on her bike, and began to float slowly home.

Grade yourself or a friend—*Graveyard School* style!

Class	Grade
Advanced Screaming	_____
Weird Science	_____
Coffin Carpentry	_____
Spooking for Beginners	_____
House Haunting	_____
Grave Digging	_____
Multiplication for Little Monsters	_____

Key to Grades:

A = Alarming
B = Beastly
C = Creepy
D = Downright Disgusting
F = Fully Frightening

Fill in the blanks. Choose from the word lists or make up your own!

Comments:

_____ has been a _____
(your name or friend's name)   (adjective)

student. So far _____ has learned
                          (name)

the importance of _____ and is
                          (plural noun)

especially _____ at _____.
              (adjective)   (plural noun)

_____works well with _____
              (name)   (plural noun)

but needs improvement with _____.
                                    (plural noun)

I have not seen such a _____
                                        (adjective)

student in years.

Sincerely,

Dr. D. Morthouse
Principal   *(Turn page for word lists)*

Word Lists

Adjectives:
Horrible
Ashen
Vile
Scary
Ugly
Slimy
Gross

Plural Nouns:
Fangs
Ghosts
Broomsticks
Witches
Warts
Bats
Spiderwebs

TILL YOU

With each and every one of these scary, creepy, delightfully, frightfully funny books, you'll be dying to go to the *Graveyard School!*

Order any or all of the books in this scary new series by **Tom B. Stone!** Just check off the titles you want, then fill out and mail the order form below.

☐ 0-553-48223-8	**DON'T EAT THE MYSTERY MEAT!**	$3.50/$4.50 Can.
☐ 0-553-48224-6	**THE SKELETON ON THE SKATEBOARD**	$3.50/$4.50 Can.
☐ 0-553-48225-4	**THE HEADLESS BICYCLE RIDER**	$3.50/$4.50 Can.
☐ 0-553-48226-2	**LITTLE PET WEREWOLF**	$3.50/$4.50 Can.
☐ 0-553-48227-0	**REVENGE OF THE DINOSAURS**	$3.50/$4.50 Can.

BDD
Bantam Doubleday Dell
Books For Young Readers

BDD BOOKS FOR YOUNG READERS
2451 South Wolf Road
Des Plaines, IL 60018

Please send me the items I have checked above. I am enclosing $_____
(please add $2.50 to cover postage and handling).
Send check or money order, no cash or C.O.D.s please.

NAME _____

ADDRESS _____

CITY _____ STATE _____ ZIP _____

Please allow four to six weeks for delivery.
Prices and availability subject to change without notice.   BFYR 113 2/95

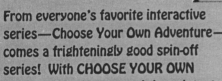